COMING TO AMERICA

THE STORY OF IMMIGRATION

BY BETSY MAESTRO

ILLUSTRATED BY
SUSANNAH RYAN

SCHOLASTIC INC.

New York Toronto London Auckland Sydney

America is a nation of immigrants. Immigrants are people who come to a new land to make their home. All Americans are related to immigrants or are immigrants themselves.

Thousands and thousands of years ago, there were no people at all in the Americas. Then, during the last great Ice Age, nomads crossed over a land bridge from Asia to what is now Alaska. These early hunters wandered here more or less by accident, searching for food.

American Indians, called "Native Americans," are distant relatives of the ancient hunters who arrived in North America so very long ago. They were the first immigrants to arrive in what was truly a new world.

As many more thousands of years passed, the descendants of the first hunters moved around North and South America. They settled in small villages and later built big cities.

By the time Christopher Columbus "discovered" America in 1492, millions of people lived in the great civilizations of the Americas.

After Columbus crossed the Atlantic Ocean, other European explorers came in search of land and riches for their own countries. Stories about the fascinating "New World" spread throughout Europe. In time, settlers followed the explorers' routes across the great ocean.

These European immigrants came to make new homes in the Americas. They came in search of a better life — one free of the trouble and hardship they had left behind. In their native countries, they often had little money and could not worship God in the way they wished. The immigrants hoped for freedom and good fortune in their new lives.

By about 1700, thousands of settlers lived in the Spanish, French, and English colonies of North America. Other new Americans had arrived from the Netherlands, Sweden, Germany, Finland, and Wales. As the population grew, the Europeans competed with the Indians for land and food. The Indians were pushed off their land and were often treated badly or killed.

Not all immigrants came to America because they wanted to. Beginning in 1619, millions of Africans were brought to the Americas against their will and were forced into slavery. Instead of finding freedom, these Africans lost theirs, and most never returned to their homelands, so very far away.

During the 1700s, settlers continued to come to the American colonies. Scotch-Irish and Swiss settlers came, too, in search of a better life, wanting to have land of their own and enough food to fill their hungry stomachs.

Their hopes for the future gave the immigrants courage to face the long and difficult sea voyage. Early sailing ships took months to cross the Atlantic Ocean. The living space was very cramped, and often there wasn't enough food or water. Stormy seas made ship-board life even more miserable.

New arrivals sometimes settled near the ports where they first landed. New York, Boston, Philadelphia, Charleston, Baltimore, and New Orleans were all growing cities. As early as 1700, about eighteen languages could be heard in the streets of New York City.

People who had come from the same country usually stayed together. They felt more at home near others who lived as they did and spoke the same language. Their new lives were very hard at first. They had little money to afford anything except the most basic necessities.

Toward the middle of the 1800s, other adventurous newcomers became part of the westward movement. After arriving in the United States, they traveled on, by boat, train, and wagon. They headed for new frontiers in the Midwest and the Great Lakes region. Free land was offered to those who would agree to stay and farm. Norwegians joined other hardy settlers and founded farming communities in places like Minnesota and Wisconsin.

Soon other pioneers moved even further west — all the way to California, where Chinese and Mexican immigrants had already settled. These early Chinese settlers helped to build the first transcontinental railroad, and when it was completed in 1869, westward travel increased. The United States had become a vast nation, spreading from the Atlantic to the Pacific Ocean.

For more than two hundred years, most immigrants had come from northern Europe and Scandinavia. By the end of the 1800s, more modern steamships had shortened the long transatlantic voyage. People began to arrive in the United States from all over the world in greater numbers. They came from Italy and Poland, Turkey and Greece, Hungary and Serbia.

Although life was hard for new immigrants, it still was better than the perils and poverty they faced in their native countries. So immigrants continued to come to the United States. Thousands poured into the many ports, from New York City to San Francisco, every year.

Before 1820, no one had recorded the exact number of immigrants who had arrived in the United States. But the numbers of immigrants were growing so rapidly that some states passed their own immigration laws to keep track of the newcomers. In 1875, the United States government began to regulate immigration. It wanted to know more about the people who were arriving daily on American shores. A number of years later, the government began to limit immigration by saying that people from some countries could not come to the United States at all.

Between 1855 and 1890, Castle Garden in New York City served as a depot for immigration. More than eight million people passed through this port of entry. A few years later, on January 1, 1892, the United States government opened an immigration center on Ellis Island near New York City. Officials from the island would count and question the new arrivals. They would see that those admitted were healthy and ready to become useful citizens.

On the day that Ellis Island opened, the first person to step ashore was Annie Moore. She was a fifteen-year-old girl from Ireland. She had traveled with her two brothers to join their parents, who had settled in the United States three years earlier.

As big passenger ships entered New York harbor, the immigrants caught their first glimpse of what they hoped would be their new country. They saw the Statue of Liberty, a welcome and inspiring sight. The travelers were relieved that their journey was over, but they worried about what awaited them on Ellis Island.

Inspectors from the island boarded the ships at anchor to check the passengers. Wealthy passengers traveling first class were usually allowed to leave the ship right away. The inspectors looked for signs of contagious disease among the others. Those who were ill sometimes stayed aboard the ship or were sent to other islands to recover. Those who seemed healthy were taken to Ellis Island.

On the busiest days, so many ships arrived in New York harbor that there were long waits just to get to Ellis Island. Sometimes the wait was so long that people had to live aboard ship for a few extra days. Once on the island, there was more waiting! With thousands arriving each day, long lines formed everywhere.

First, the immigrants were given a quick examination by doctors. Those with health problems were marked with colored chalk. The doctors would examine these persons more closely. Some people were kept on the island for observation. After 1911, Ellis Island had its own hospital to treat the sick.

Sometimes immigrants had permanent health problems that would make it hard for them to work. This often meant that they would be sent back to their native country. But most of the new arrivals passed inspection and moved on to the next step.

Now, the immigrants were asked a long list of questions. Inspectors asked their names, where they were from, and how much money they had. Since most of the immigrants did not speak English, they needed help in understanding and answering the questions. Translators did what they could to help the inspectors and newcomers understand one another.

Even though it was difficult, most managed somehow to answer all the questions. Mothers often spoke for children who might be too little or too scared to speak. The immigrants had to show that they would work hard and stay out of trouble. Usually the ordeal was over within the day. When they received their entry cards, at last, the immigrants could officially enter their new country.

During the busy years at Ellis Island, millions of immigrants passed through its massive halls. World War I slowed the huge flow of people into the United States. In 1921, the United States government passed more laws limiting the number of people who could enter the country. These laws were unfair and were later changed.

Other laws were passed requiring new immigrants to have medical examinations before boarding ships in foreign ports. As a result, Ellis Island was no longer very busy, and finally, in 1954, it was closed. In 1990, Ellis Island was reopened as a museum. Today, most immigrants no longer arrive by ship. Instead, they fly into the many international airports in the United States.

All newcomers to America have a hard time at first. This is true whether they came in the 1600s or have just arrived. It isn't easy to start a new life in an unfamiliar country. Most immigrants have to learn a new language and a new way of life. The jobs they must take are often hard, with long hours. Sadly, new arrivals are often poorly treated by other Americans just because they look or act differently.

New Americans make their lives a little better by finding friends from their native country. As they have in the past, immigrants often group together in small neighborhoods. It helps them to feel more at home in a strange, new country. Many different languages can be heard on the streets of the ethnic neighborhoods in big cities.

Many people who come to the United States are refugees. These people are forced to leave their homelands to escape persecution or the dangers of war and natural disaster. From its beginning, the United States has taken in countless refugees from countries all over the world.

After World War II, refugees from Europe arrived on our shores. In more recent years, Southeast Asian, Cuban, and Haitian refugees have fled from homes where they could no longer be safe. They seek protection and shelter in the United States.

Today's new immigrants have come to the United States from Russia, Asia, Mexico, South and Central America, the Middle East, the West Indies, and Africa. They are still coming for the same reason people have always come — to make a better life for themselves and for their children.

America has been called a great "melting pot," where many cultures, or ways of life, have blended together. But today, Americans have also learned to celebrate their differences. There is a growing appreciation and understanding of the special character and unique contributions of each cultural or ethnic group. Everyone, from the first Americans thousands of years ago to those who came only yesterday, has left a lasting mark on this great land.

Immigrants settled and farmed this land before it was a country. Others created a new nation and founded its government. Immigrants built the cities, roads, and railways of America. They have toiled in its fields, its factories, and its mills. Immigrants, too, have made the music of this land, written its books, and recorded its beauty in paintings. The spirit of American strength and independence is the spirit of its people — the spirit of its immigrants and their children.

TABLE OF DATES

About 20,000 BC First people come to North America from Asia.

AD 200 Civilizations flourish in the Americas.

1000 Vikings settle for a short time in Newfoundland, Canada.

1492 Columbus reaches the Americas. Other European explorers soon follow.

1505 First African slaves are brought to the Americas by the Spaniards.

1537 New Spain is established in Mexico after conquest of Aztecs.

1541 French explorer Jacques Cartier founds settlement at Quebec, Canada.

1565 Spanish establish fort at San Agustìn, later St. Augustine, Florida.

1585 English settle briefly on Roanoke Island, off North Carolina.

1607 First permanent English colony is established at Jamestown, Virginia.

1619 First African slaves are brought to the English colonies.

1620 Pilgrims come to Massachusetts in search of religious freedom.

1624 Dutch settle in New Amsterdam, later New York City.

1630 Puritans come to Massachusetts; 16,000 come to Boston in next 10 years.

1638 First Swedes come to Delaware.

1640 Colonial population is about 28,000.

1677 Quakers arrive from England.

1683 Welsh and Germans settle near Philadelphia.

1709 Swiss and German immigrants settle in the Carolinas.

1718 New Orleans is founded by the French.

1750 Population numbers over one million.

1769 Spanish establish first mission in California.

1790 First census, or counting of citizens, is authorized by Congress. Population reaches almost 4 million.

1821 First American settlement is founded in Texas, at Austin.

1845 Thousands of Irish begin coming to escape famine in Ireland.

1848 First Chinese immigrants arrive in San Francisco.

1850 The seventh U.S. Census counts about 23 million in the 31 states of the union.

1886 The Statue of Liberty is unveiled.

1892 Ellis Island opens.

1900 U.S. population stands at 76 million. There are 45 states.

1907 Peak year for Ellis Island. More than one million immigrants pass through.

1917 Thirty-three different groups are now excluded from coming to America.

1950 U.S. population is now about 150 million. There are 48 states.

1954 Ellis Island closes.

1965-1992 New immigration laws end discriminatory quotas, set numerical limits, and offer amnesty to many illegal immigrants.

2000 Population is more than 260 million.

IMMIGRATION TODAY

Before 1965, there were limits on the numbers of immigrants who could come to the United States from many countries. These quotas, based on national origin, were abolished by the Immigration and Nationality Act of 1965. The United States began to give preference to those who were refugees and those who already had family members in the country. Between 1981 and 1990, more than seven million immigrants were admitted. Most of the new citizens were Asians and Hispanics.

Today, nearly one million legal immigrants arrive in the United States each year. Many others enter the country illegally. These immigrants do not have permission to come. Because they are often desperate to leave political unrest or economic hardship at home, they take great risks, traveling by boat or coming across the border with Mexico. Smugglers sometimes "help" these illegal aliens to get into the United States. The cost is very high — some die in transit, and many others find themselves virtual slaves when they reach their destination. Although the government tries to intervene, illegal immigration is hard to control.

OTHER INTERESTING FACTS ABOUT IMMIGRATION

In 1654, Jewish refugees arrived in New Amsterdam. They hoped to find religious freedom in America after fleeing intolerance and violence in Spain.

In 1755, during the French and Indian Wars, the British deported French settlers from Nova Scotia. About 900 Acadian refugees arrived in the American colonies.

Early in the 1800s, it was not unusual for one tenth of the passengers aboard ship to die during the long ocean voyage. Often, more than half the passengers were ill.

The length of time for an ocean crossing changed from around 15 weeks in the middle of the 1700s to about 15 days by 1840.

About 30 different languages were spoken by the staff and officials of Ellis Island.

More than 20 million immigrants came to the United States between 1880 and 1920.

In 1897, a fire destroyed the five-year-old immigration center on Ellis Island. In 1900, a new, fireproof center opened. By 1914 there were 33 buildings, including a chapel, hospital, and laundry.

About 10 million Africans were brought to the Americas as slaves. Most African-Americans are their descendants.

Over 100 million Americans, two fifths of our population, can trace their roots to a relative who passed through Ellis Island.

Thousands of newly arrived immigrants settle in New York City every year. More than 100 different languages are spoken there.

For Sam
— B.M.

For David Penn and Adam Stires
— S.R.

ISBN 0-590-44152-3

Text copyright © 1996 by Betsy Maestro.
Illustrations copyright © 1996 by Susannah Ryan.
All rights reserved. Published by Scholastic Inc.

25 24 23 22 21 20 19 18   08 09 10
Printed in the U.S.A.   40

The illustrations in this book are watercolor paintings.
Production supervision by Angela Biola
Designed by Claire B. Counihan